The Penguin Book

Amanda Miller

Brought to you by the editors of

My Weekly Reader

Children's Press®
An imprint of Scholastic Inc.

How to Read This Book

This book is for kids and grown-ups to read together—side by side!

A 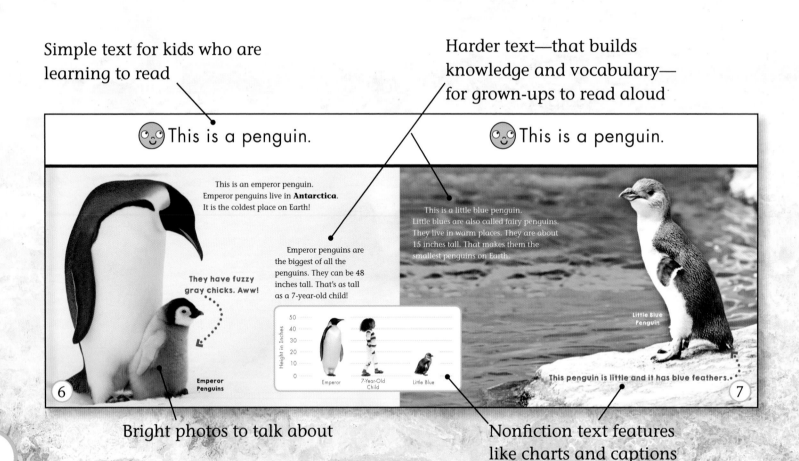 means it is the kid's turn to read.

A grown-up can read the rest.

Simple text for kids who are learning to read

Harder text—that builds knowledge and vocabulary—for grown-ups to read aloud

This is a penguin.

This is a penguin.

This is an emperor penguin. Emperor penguins live in **Antarctica**. It is the coldest place on Earth!

They have fuzzy gray chicks. Aww!

Emperor penguins are the biggest of all the penguins. They can be 48 inches tall. That's as tall as a 7-year-old child!

This is a little blue penguin. Little blues are also called fairy penguins. They live in warm places. They are about 15 inches tall. That makes them the smallest penguins on Earth.

Little Blue Penguin

Emperor Penguins

Height in Inches
50
40
30
20
10
0

Emperor   7-Year-Old Child   Little Blue

This penguin is little and it has blue feathers.

6

7

Bright photos to talk about

Nonfiction text features like charts and captions

Table of Contents

Emperor

Gentoo

Chinstrap

Chapter 1

All Kinds of Penguins

There are many kinds of penguins. Let's meet some of them!

Macaroni   **Adélie**   **Rockhopper**   **Little Blue**

 This is a penguin.

This is an emperor penguin. Emperor penguins live in **Antarctica**. It is the coldest place on Earth!

Emperor penguins are the biggest of all the penguins. They can be 48 inches tall. That's as tall as a 7-year-old child!

They have fuzzy gray chicks. Aww!

Emperor Penguins

Height in Inches

50

40

30

20

10

0

Emperor

7-Year-Old Child

6

This is a penguin.

This is a little blue penguin. Little blues are also called fairy penguins. They live in warm places. They are about 5 inches tall. That makes them the smallest penguins on Earth.

Little Blue
Penguin

Little Blue

This penguin is little and it has blue feathers.

☺ This is a penguin.

This is a chinstrap penguin. Chinstraps have a line of black **feathers** on their chin. Can you point to the line on this penguin? The line looks like the strap for a helmet or a hat. That's how these penguins got the name chinstrap!

Chinstrap Penguin

Chinstraps make nests out of rocks.

egg

8

This is a penguin.

These are Adélie (uh-DAY-lee) penguins. If you want to know if a penguin is an Adélie, look at its eyes. Adélie penguins are the only penguins that have a white ring around their eyes.

This is what Adélie chicks look like!

Adélie Penguins

This is a penguin too.

These are rockhopper penguins. They live on rocky beaches and **cliffs**. They are great at hopping and climbing.

Rockhopper Penguin

The bunch of spiky feathers on a rockhopper's head is called a crest.

Rockhoppers have bright-red eyes. They have pink webbed feet.

Chapter 2

Go, Go, Penguins!

Penguins are birds, but they can't fly. How do they get around?

King Penguins

Penguins can walk.

Penguins **waddle** when they walk. They lean from side to side as they walk on their short legs. They use their claws to grip the ice.

When penguins are tired of waddling, they flop onto their bellies and slide on the ice.

Emperor Penguins

12

Penguins can hop.

How else do they get around?
Some penguins are fantastic hoppers.
They hop from rock to rock.

Gentoo Penguin

13

Penguins can swim.

Penguins are excellent swimmers. They look like they are flying underwater. They flap their flippers and use their **webbed feet**.

flippers

King Penguin

claws

webbed feet

bill

belly

Penguins catch food in the water. They don't have teeth to chew. They swallow their food whole. Gulp!

14

What Most Penguins Eat

krill	fish	squid

Chapter 3

Penguin Chick Grows Up

From egg to adult—let's find out how an emperor penguin grows.

Emperor Penguin Chicks

This is a penguin egg.

Female emperor penguins lay only one egg every year. The mother penguin passes the egg to the father penguin. He takes care of the egg while the mother penguin goes fishing in the sea.

The father penguin keeps the egg warm and safe on his feet.

This penguin egg is hatching.

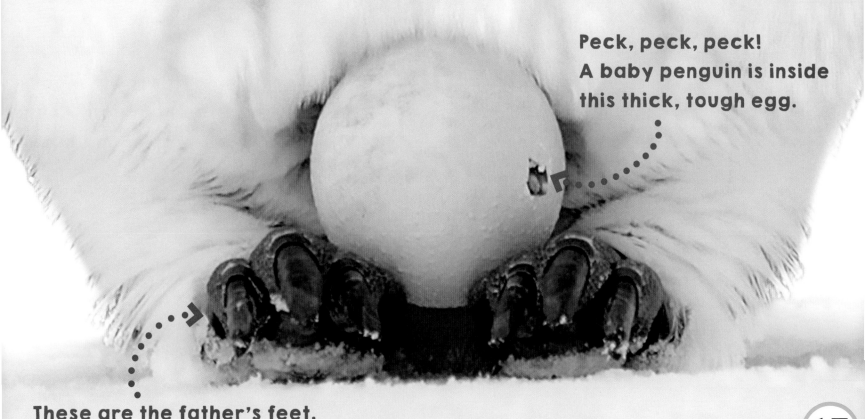

The penguin chick pokes a hole with its beak from the inside of the egg. When the shell is broken, the chick **hatches**!

Peck, peck, peck! A baby penguin is inside this thick, tough egg.

These are the father's feet.

☺ This is a penguin chick.

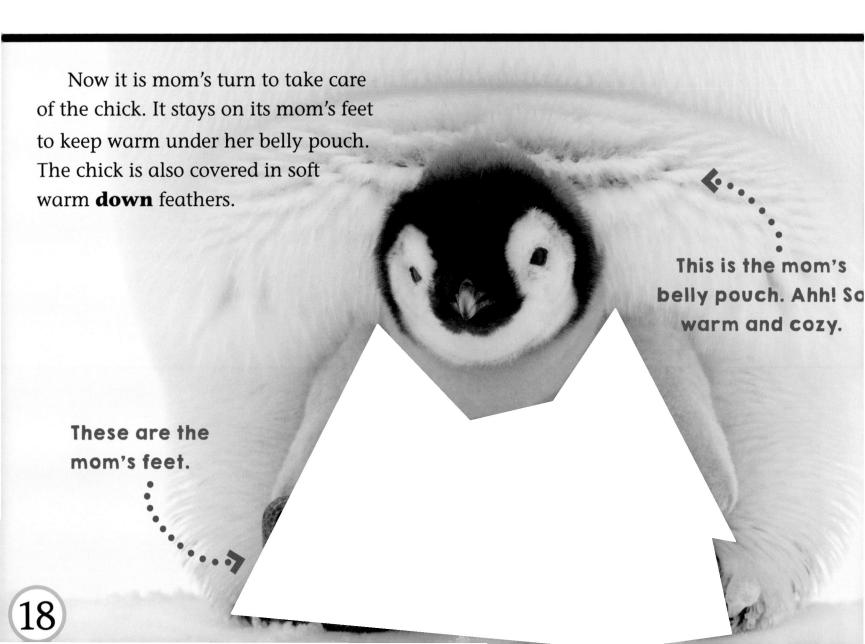

Now it is mom's turn to take care of the chick. It stays on its mom's feet to keep warm under her belly pouch. The chick is also covered in soft warm **down** feathers.

This is the mom's belly pouch. Ahh! So warm and cozy.

These are the mom's feet.

18

This penguin chick is eating.

The penguin chick can't catch its own food. The parents take turns feeding it.

The mom spits up fish into the chick's mouth.

When their parents are out fishing at sea, the chicks huddle together to keep warm.

A huddle of penguin chicks is called a crèche.

This penguin chick is growing.

The chick gets bigger and bigger. When it's 5 months old, it loses its soft down and grows new feathers. This is called **molting**.

When the chick has all its new feathers, it will be ready to go fishing in the sea.

The new feathers are waterproof for swimming

This penguin is all grown up!

Now the chick is all grown up. It goes out to sea to eat fish and fatten up. One day, it might have its own chick to take care of.

How a Penguin Grows

egg   chick   molting chick   adult

21

Glossary

Antarctica: (ant-**ark**-ti-kah)

The cold, snowy continent around the South Pole

cliff: (klif)

A high, steep rock face

down: (down)

The soft, fuzzy feathers of a baby bird

feathers: (**feth**-urz)

Soft, fluffy parts that cover a bird's body

hatch:
(hach)
To break out
of an egg

waddle:
(**wad**-uhl)
To lean from side to
side while walking

new
feathers

molt: (mohlt)
To shed feathers
so new feathers
can grow

web

webbed feet: (webd feet)
Feet with skin between the toes,
like a duck's feet

23

Index

Adélie penguin   5, 9

adult   21

Antarctica   6

belly   12, 14, 18

bill   14

body   14

chick   6, 9, 15, 18, 19, 20, 21

chinstrap penguin   4, 8

claws   12, 14

cliffs   10

crèche   19

down   18, 20

egg   16, 17, 21

emperor penguin   4, 6, 12, 15, 16

eyes   9, 10

fairy penguin, see little blue penguin

feathers   8, 10, 18, 20

feet   10, 14, 16, 17, 18

flippers   14

food   14, 19

gentoo penguin   4, 13

hatching   17

hopping   10, 13

huddling   19

king penguins   11, 14

life cycle   15-21

little blue penguin (fairy penguin)   5, 7

macaroni penguin   5

molting   20, 21

movement, kinds of   11-14

nest   8

parents   16, 17, 18, 19

rockhopper penguin   5, 10

size   6-7

sliding   12

swimming   14, 20, 21

waddling   12

Photographs ©: cover main: Stephen Belcher/Minden Pictures; cover smiley faces and throughout: Giuseppe_R/Shutterstock; back cover: Martin Ruegner/Photographer's Choice/Getty Images; 2 background: photosoft/Shutterstock; 3: vladsilver/Shutterstock; 4 left: Jan Martin Will/Shutterstock; 4 center: javarman/Shutterstock; 4 right: Joe & Mary McDonald/Kimball Stock; 5 left: Leksele/Shutterstock; 5 center left: Leksele/Shutterstock; 5 center right: Tui De Roy/Minden Pictures; 5 right: GoodOlga/Panther Media GmbH/Alamy Images; 6 main: Hiroya Minakuchi/Minden Pictures; 6 inset right: Photoeuphoria/Dreamstime; 6 inset left: Jan Martin Will/Shutterstock; 7 main: Khoroshunova Olga/Shutterstock; 7 inset: GoodOlga/Panther Media GmbH/Alamy Images; 8: Sylvain Cordier/Minden Pictures; 9 inset: robert mcgillivray/Shutterstock; 9 main: Suzi Eszterhas/Minden Pictures; 10 background: Pipochka/Shutterstock; 10 left: Solvin Zankl/Minden Pictures; 10 right: Tui D Roy/Minden Pictures; 11: Klein-Hubert/Kimball Stock; 12 inset: Klein-Hubert/Kimball Stock; 12 main: Martin Ragner/Westend61/Alamy Images; 12 left penguin: Keren Su/China Span/Alamy Images; 13: Charlie Summers/Minden Pictures; 14 center: Hiroya Minakuchi/Minden Pictures; 14 inset left: British Antarctic Survey/Science Source; 14 inset center: Opas Chotiphantawanon/Shutterstock; 14 inset right: JIANG HONGYAN/Shutterstock; 15: Klein and Hubert/Minden Pictures; 16 main: Stefan Christmann/Minden Pictures; 16 inset: The Natural History Museum/Alamy Images; 17: Fred Olivier/Nature Picture Library; 18: Rob Reijnen/Minden Pictures; 19 main: Pete Oxford/Nature Picture Library; 19 inset: Stefan Christmann/Minden Pictures; 20 main: Tim Davis/Corbis/Getty Images; 20 inset: Stefan Christmann/Minden Pictures; 21 top: Keren Su/Photodisc/Getty Images; 21 bottom center left: Bryan and Cherry Alexander/Nature Picture Library; 21 bottom right: Jan Martin Will/Shutterstock; 21 bottom left: The Natural History Museum/Alamy Images; 21 bottom center right: Stefan Christmann/Minden Pictures; 22 bottom left: JeremyRichards/Shutterstock; 22 top right: Klein Hubert/Kimball Stock; 22 bottom right white feather: ILYA AKINSHIN/Shutterstock; 22 bottom right black feather: errorfoto/Shutterstock; 22 top left: Pyty/Shutterstock; 23 top left: Solvin Zankl/Minden Pictures; 23 bottom right: Yva Momatiuk and John Eastcott/Minden Pictures; 23 bottom left: Stefan Christmann/Minden Pictures; 23 top center: Martin Ragner/Westend61/Alamy Images; 23 top right: Keren Su/China Span/Alamy Images.

Library of Congress Cataloging-in-Publication Data

Names: Miller, Amanda, author.
Title: The penguin book / by Amanda Miller.
Description: New York, NY : Children's Press, an imprint of Scholastic Inc., 2019. | Series: Side by side | Includes index.
Identifiers: LCCN 2018029942| ISBN 9780531131091 (library binding) | ISBN 9780531136478 (paperback)
Subjects: LCSH: Penguins--Juvenile literature.
Classification: LCC QL696.S47 M55 2019 | DDC 598.47--dc23

Brought to you by the editors of Let's Find Out®. Original Design by Joan Michael and Judith E. Christ for Scholastic Inc.